Beauty & the Beast

Jeanne-Marie Leprince de Beaumont

As retold by Mahlon F. Craft

and Illustrated by

KINUKO Y. CRAFT

HARPER

An Imprint of HarperCollinsPublishers

A note from the Artist and the Author

The retelling of this story is loosely themed on Jeanne-Marie Leprince de Beaumont's version first published in France in 1756. The artist's setting for the story takes place in an illusionary castle set deep in a dark forest. She reviewed Beaumont's version and numerous other retellings, searching for fragments of the tale from which she could bring to life visually rich and imaginative scenes. The author then undertook the task of weaving those scenes together in his own words, creating the new retelling appearing herein for the first time. Each of the many intricate works reproduced in this book was created in artist's oil paint with miniature sable brushes on a gesso panel. We hope you will find them and this retelling as interesting and enjoyable as we did in creating and designing it.

Oil over watercolor on gesso panel
was used for the full-color illustrations.
The text type is 13-point
Bernhard Roman BT, with 6-point leading.

ISBN 978-0-06-053919-1

Typography by Jeanne Hogle
16 17 18 19 20   SCP   10 9 8 7 6 5 4 3 2 1
❖
First Edition

For Jacqueline

nce upon a time, there lived a wealthy merchant who had three daughters. He doted lovingly on them, giving them the finest education and every advantage money could buy.

The youngest daughter possessed a lovely fairness so rare that everyone came to call her Beauty even while she was still a little child. She was not only far more beautiful than her two elder sisters, but she was also generous and kindhearted in nature.

But despite her kind nature, the two elder daughters were jealous of Beauty in the extreme. Beauty had a great many marriage proposals, but as she loved her father dearly, she always gently refused, saying she felt herself yet too young to leave his house.

Then one day a great misfortune befell the merchant. He lost his entire fortune and everything he owned, save a small cottage in the country. The family was forced to move there and survive by the work of their own hands.

pon arriving at their cottage, Beauty immediately set about cleaning and placing the house in order. She rose every day at four o'clock to begin her work. Her sisters, on the other hand, slept until noon and lifted not a finger.

At first, Beauty sometimes cried in secret, so despairing of the hardships they had to suffer. But eventually she mastered her new chores and found the time to read or play her harp. She became content and, by the hard work, ever more radiant and beautiful.

A year or so later, a letter arrived. When her father read it, he nearly shouted for joy. "We are saved!" he cried. "My ship, long thought lost, has come into port with all its rich cargo intact. Our labors are over!"

At this news, Beauty's elder sisters grew excited and begged their father to buy them new clothes and jewelry with the money he would receive from the goods on the ship. But Beauty asked for nothing, and this troubled her father. "Is there not something that I can bring for you?" he asked.

Finally Beauty replied simply, "I should be very happy if you could bring me a rose. We have none in our garden and it would so brighten our table."

hen the merchant arrived at his ship, he found everything was being held to pay his debts. He was forced to set out for home as poor as he had left.

On the way back, his horse took a wrong turn and he found himself lost in a dense forest. A bitterly cold wind sprang up, and it began to snow. Night fell, but after a short time the storm eased a little and a path appeared in the gloom. Almost as soon as he had ventured a few steps down it, the snow stopped and the air became fresh and sweet. He found himself on a broad avenue lined with flowering orange trees covered with fruit. At the end of it a magnificent castle rose up, its gate standing open, and when the merchant passed through he found well-tended gardens but not a soul in sight. There was also a large stable, and his horse went into it without the slightest hesitation.

Entering the castle, the merchant found himself in a large hall, where food and drink were laid out and a place was set. When eleven o'clock passed and yet no one came to greet him, the sight of the food became too much for the poor, tired man.

"I'm sorry for any rudeness to my host," he thought, then sat down and ate his fill.

When by midnight his host still had not appeared, the merchant thought he might as well see what else the place held for him. Opening a door at the end of a hall, he found a luxurious bedchamber with a fire blazing and a comfortable bed turned down waiting for him. There he lay down and fell fast asleep.

he merchant awakened to find a handsome new set of clothes laid out for him, and on the table a hot breakfast stood waiting. "Surely this is magic and some good fairy has taken pity on my misfortune," he thought. "I thank you whoever you are, but now I must be off to my family."

On his way to the stables the good merchant passed under a rose arbor.

"Surely this good fairy will not begrudge me a rose for Beauty," he said. But as soon as he had plucked it from its stem, a terrible voice rang out:

"Ungrateful man!"

Then appeared the most hideous and frightful creature the merchant had ever seen. "How dare you repay my kindness by stealing that which I prize above all else! You must pay for your crime with your life!"

"Please, my lord!" begged the merchant. "I took the rose only to fulfill an innocent daughter's wish. For this surely I do not deserve to die!"

The creature thought for a moment and said, "Daughters, you say? If one will come in your place, you may escape your fate. But if not, you must promise to return in three months."

The merchant gave his word but without the slightest intention of asking any one of his daughters to die in his stead. "At least I shall see my children again," he thought.

But then the Beast spoke once more. "I do not wish you to return to your family with nothing to show for your journey. In the room where you slept you will find an empty chest. Fill it with whatever you like from my castle and I will have it delivered to you." Then the Beast turned and left.

"And so," sighed the merchant, "I must be eaten by the Beast and die. But at least I can leave my children with some good fortune." He found the chest just as the Beast had told him and filled it with gold coins and jewels till it could hold no more. Then he locked it and left it behind.

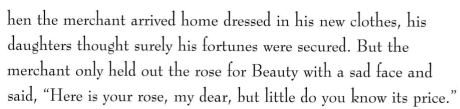hen the merchant arrived home dressed in his new clothes, his daughters thought surely his fortunes were secured. But the merchant only held out the rose for Beauty with a sad face and said, "Here is your rose, my dear, but little do you know its price." Then the merchant began to sob and told everything that had come to pass.

"Look what you have done!" the two elder sisters shouted at Beauty. "If you had wished for such things as we had instead of your stupid rose, this never would have happened. Now you will be the cause of our father's death!"

"No," Beauty said, "Father shall not die. Since it was I whose wish has caused this misfortune, it is I who must go to the Beast."

No matter how he argued, the merchant could not dissuade Beauty from her choice. This, of course, made the two elder sisters quite glad, for they had always hated how everyone loved Beauty more than them.

That night, to his great surprise, the merchant found the chest promised by the Beast next to his bed, which he immediately hid. He told only Beauty of this so she would not worry, fearing his two elder daughters would squander the treasure.

Three months passed quickly. When the appointed day arrived, Beauty was awakened by the sound of heavy hooves and neighing. As she opened the door of the cottage, a magnificent horse stood waiting, pawing at the ground with his hoof. It was time for Beauty to say good-bye.

The two elder sisters rubbed their eyes with onions to make everyone think they were crying. The merchant's eyes were so wet he could hardly see. Only Beauty's eyes were dry, for she was determined to be brave for her father's sake.

Beauty climbed onto Splendid (for that was the horse's name), and before she could say a word the horse was at a gallop, with his hooves barely touching the earth.

In just a few hours they reached the castle. There she found a table laid out with a sumptuous feast. She decided to eat, though she was sure the Beast meant only to fatten her up before killing and eating her.

Just as Beauty finished her supper, the clock struck ten. A door opened. Though what Beauty now saw made her tremble in fear, she stood up and bowed her head.

"Good evening," said the Beast.

This surprised Beauty, who had expected the creature to be anything but polite. "Good evening," she answered. "I am Beauty, come in my father's place."

"It is well that you are here of your own accord," the Beast replied. "Your father has a loving daughter. Now I bid you good evening."

"Good night," said Beauty, and with that, the Beast turned and left.

Exhausted, Beauty soon fell asleep where she sat. In her dream, a faerie appeared who said, "Dear Beauty, fear nothing; your courage will soon be rewarded."

When the clock next struck, Beauty awakened. She found a sign that read "This way to Beauty's room!" pointing to a door. Taking courage, Beauty opened the door, and after a short distance she came to another. Behind it, she found the most splendid chamber she had ever seen. On a small table she found a book lying open with these verses written in gold:

> Lovely Beauty, dry your eyes.
> In this place no danger lies,
> For when you have a wish or need,
> You have only to ask and I must heed.

Now Beauty could not help thinking of her father. "Oh, how I wish I could see him once more." She sighed. At that moment, a looking glass that rested on the table turned over and faced her. In it, she saw her father in his chair fast asleep by the fire. Then just as quickly, the image faded. By this she saw that the Beast, though terrible in form, perhaps had a kind heart.

he next evening, when she was about to begin her supper, again she heard the approach of the Beast. Still not knowing what he intended for her, Beauty could not help being greatly afraid.

"Good evening Beauty. May I sit with you while you dine?" he asked.

"If that is your wish, I cannot refuse," Beauty answered.

"Dear Beauty," the Beast replied, "it is your wishes I must follow. I will leave immediately if my presence offends you, but pray tell: Do you not think I am very ugly?"

"Indeed you are," said Beauty, "but though I am also very afraid of you, you have shown me that part of you is not so fearsome as you appear."

"Perhaps," answered the Beast, "but I am an evil monster all the same."

"I would far rather know a monster such as you than many a monster I know who appear human in form," Beauty replied quite honestly.

A soft sadness somehow came to the Beast's face after Beauty spoke these words, which made her fear nearly disappear. They sat talking while Beauty ate, and by the end of supper she had almost forgotten that she sat with a beast at her table.

When the clock struck ten, the Beast rose to depart and then quite without warning asked, "Beauty, will you marry me?"

Quite shocked and once again frightened, she answered simply, "I cannot."

The Beast sighed and left without uttering a word.

Each day thereafter, the Beast provided some new wonder for Beauty's amusement. There was an aviary full of birds, all so tame they perched on her shoulders, and cockatoos who even called her by name. The garden seemed to change every day, and new paths appeared with fresh delights. She even found a room in the castle where plays were presented, dancers performed, and musicians played at her command whenever she wished.

hree months passed this way. Each night, through Beauty's conversations with the Beast, she found some new good thing in him. Gradually Beauty came to look forward to nine o'clock when, without fail, he arrived every evening. Also without fail, every evening he asked for her hand in marriage before saying good night.

At last Beauty could stand this no longer. "Please don't force me to refuse you so often," she said softly. "I will always be your friend, but I do not think I will ever desire to be your wife."

"I know how terrible I am to look at," replied the Beast. "But I love you almost more than life itself. Please promise that you will never leave me."

This plea by the Beast caused Beauty finally to break down. Only that day her magic looking glass had shown her father lying gravely ill in his bed.

"I must see my father," Beauty sobbed, "and if you will not allow it, my heart will break."

Beauty's streaming tears nearly broke the Beast's heart in two. "Tomorrow I will send you to your father's cottage. You need not return. It is my heart that must break even if I must die of grief."

But Beauty found that something far deeper than friendship for the Beast had come into her heart. "I cannot be the cause of your death," she said, "but my father is now ill and all alone. Please allow me to stay a week with him and then I will return." Then Beauty took a locket and chain from her own neck and gave it to the Beast.

"Tomorrow morning, you will find yourself in your father's cottage. When you wish to return, twist the ring on your finger around three times and say: 'I wish to be with my Beast again.' Do not forget your promise!"

eauty awoke once again in her father's cottage. Leaping out of bed, she ran straight into his room. At the sight of her, the poor man burst into tears. "I thought never to have seen you again," he said as they embraced. "How is it that you have come here?" Beauty told all, and by this her father seemed much restored.

When Beauty returned to her room, a large chest suddenly appeared, upon which was written: "Beauty's Chest!" She found all manner of rich and beautiful dresses inside it. Even the plainest, which Beauty immediately chose, was adorned all over with gold and pearls and diamonds.

Upon hearing of her return, Beauty's sisters, who had the miserably unhappy married lives they deserved, immediately paid a visit. Seeing how Beauty was dressed, they practically burst with envy; and when Beauty told her story and how happy she had become, their jealousy and spite knew no bounds.

The two sisters then plotted to destroy Beauty's good fortune. They went into the garden and said in low whispers, "If we keep her here more than the week the Beast has allowed, perhaps he will die, or instead become so angry he will eat her up after all."

For the next week, the sisters were everything to Beauty they had never been. They dressed her in the morning, read verses to her each afternoon, kept the house, and falsely gave her the unfettered love she had always deserved. Beauty nearly burst with joy.

At the end of the week, the sisters begged Beauty to stay another, feigning so much sadness over her departure that she could not refuse. But Beauty also now felt hopelessly torn between the unexpected love her sisters had shown her and her promise to the Beast.

On the tenth night, Beauty had a terrible dream in which the Beast lay dying in a clearing at the end of a path in the forest. With his last breath he lamented, "Why have you forsaken me and not kept your promise?" Beauty awoke with her heart pounding and tears streaming down her cheeks. She finally understood that the Beast had stolen her heart and that she could no longer be apart from him.

That night, after everyone had gone to bed, Beauty left a note for her father. When she got into bed, she turned the ring on her finger around three times and whispered, "I wish to be with my Beast again," just as the Beast had said.

In the morning, to her joy, Beauty found herself once again in the castle of the Beast. After rising and dressing herself, there was nothing to do but await his arrival. "How slowly the day passes," she thought out loud, "when it is only the end of it that has any hope for me."

When finally evening came and the clock struck nine, and then the quarter hour, and the Beast still had not come, Beauty feared the worst. She ran from room to room, calling out his name, but the only answer was stillness and silence. "Oh, dear Beast," she shouted, sobbing, "have I lost you forever?"

In her desperation, Beauty finally remembered the path from her dream. When she got to the end of it, there she found the Beast, lying lifelessly next to a fountain.

With tears welling in her eyes, she threw herself on the Beast. He stirred a little and Beauty found that his heart still beat. Cupping her hands in the fountain, she fetched water and sprinkled it over the Beast's face, whereupon he opened his eyes and spoke in a weak voice. "When you did not return, I could not bear the thought of living without you, and so I came here to starve and die. Now that I have seen your face once more, I shall leave this earth content."

"Dear Beast, you cannot die. The feeling I thought was just friendship I now know in my heart is true love. We shall marry and become husband and wife. Please live, dear Beast!" Then Beauty bent down her head and kissed the Beast tenderly on his lips.

The moment their lips touched, the castle blazed with light, and sounds of laughter and merriment could be heard. When Beauty lifted her head, she found the Beast was no more and in his place lay a handsome young prince. Startled, Beauty exclaimed, "Where is my Beast? I want him and none other!" she cried in despair.

"He is still here," replied the prince, around whose neck Beauty's locket now hung. "I was enchanted by a mischievous faerie who changed me to the form of a beast till a beautiful young woman should offer herself in marriage. Only you judged me by my heart alone. Now my heart and all that I possess are yours."

The prince then led Beauty into his castle, where a beautiful faerie appeared. With a wave of the faerie's hand, Beauty found her father and her two sisters standing in front of her.

"An honest heart," the faerie began, "is a far better thing than handsome looks or a cunning mind. You have chosen well, and the reward you long deserved is now finally yours."

Now the faerie turned to the two elder sisters. "I know of no two other people who have done such selfish and heartless deeds with so little reason. You too shall have your reward."

At that moment the two sisters were transported through the air to either side of the castle's doorway, where they instantly became stone statues. "You shall stand here until you repent for your selfishness and spite and have cured your faults. Only then may you once again regain your human form."

The faerie turned as if to leave, but she stopped and turned back. "If the truth be known," she said, "it seems to me that your present form is the one you are very likely to have forever."

When after many months the two sisters remained as stone, Beauty came to realize even her kind heart could not cure her sisters' faults. Out of pity, she had the statues moved where they could gaze on a meadow filled with wildflowers, and there to this day they remain.

As for Beauty and her Beast, they lived happy lives till the end of their days—and those were many indeed.

The End